The Scrap Doll

Also by Liz Rosenberg

Adelaide and the Night Train

Window, Mirror, Moon

The Scrap Doll

by Liz Rosenberg
pictures by Robin Ballard

A Charlotte Zolotow Book
An Imprint of HarperCollins*Publishers*

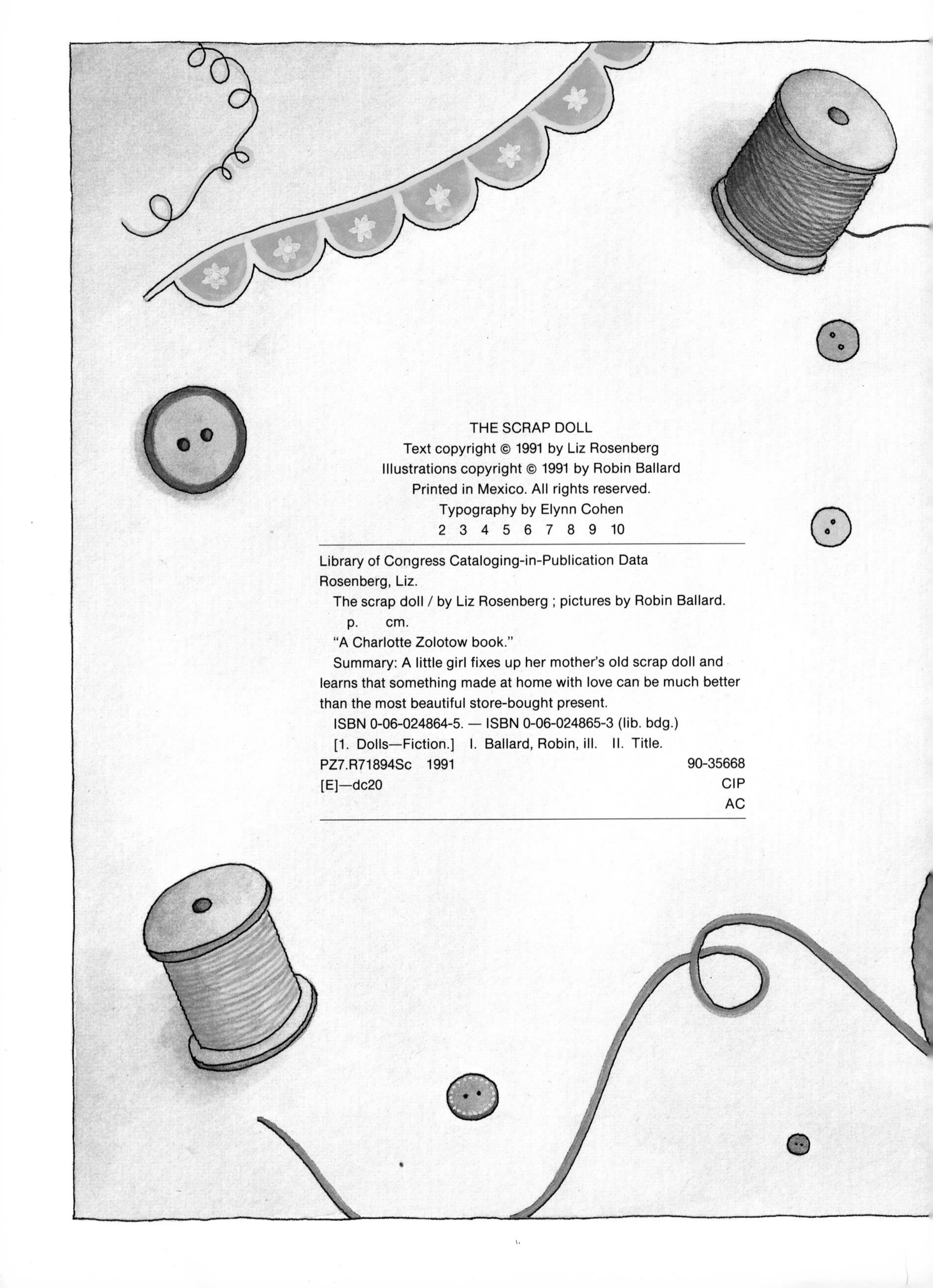

THE SCRAP DOLL

Typography by Elynn Cohen
2 3 4 5 6 7 8 9 10

Library of Congress Cataloging-in-Publication Data
Rosenberg, Liz.
The scrap doll / by Liz Rosenberg ; pictures by Robin Ballard.
p. cm.
"A Charlotte Zolotow book."
Summary: A little girl fixes up her mother's old scrap doll and learns that something made at home with love can be much better than the most beautiful store-bought present.
ISBN 0-06-024864-5. — ISBN 0-06-024865-3 (lib. bdg.)
[1. Dolls—Fiction.] I. Ballard, Robin, ill. II. Title.
PZ7.R71894Sc 1991 90-35668
[E]—dc20 CIP
AC

To my parents,
who taught me all about love
—L.R.

To Don, Priscilla, and Susie,
who have been so supportive
of me and my work
—R.B.

Lydia wanted a store-bought doll, with yellow hair and blue eyes that blinked. But there wasn't the money for any such thing.

"When I was a girl," her mother told her, "my daddy made me a doll out of scraps. Her name was Sarah, and I loved her so much."

"But I want mine store-bought," Lydia said.

"I know," said her mother. And she sounded sorry, and looked sorry.

She came down from the attic holding an old shoe box. Inside lay a scruffy-looking doll, with staring eyes and a bald head.

"That was my scrap doll," her mother said. "Why don't you fix her up a little? Name her anything you like."

Lydia felt sorry too. In her mind she called the doll Ugly Old Thing. Sarah was too pretty a name.

But she took out her paint box. She mixed her favorite shade of blue, the color of a summer sky. Then Ugly Old Thing stared back at her with bright, kindly eyes.

So Lydia painted a smiling mouth and round pink cheeks. It took a long time to get them just right. Then she laid the doll back into her shoe box. "Good night, Ugly Old Thing," she said.

THE
A
FAIRYTALE

She took the doll up again the next morning. The poor thing looked funny with her little bald head. The more she smiled, the funnier she looked.

So Lydia cut up some yellow-yarn hair. She curled the ends and added a green bow.

1 2 3 4 5 6 7 8 9 10 11 12 13 14 15 16 17 18 19 20 21

She noticed the doll had just painted-on clothes. And those clothes were rubbed thin and worn out in places. So Lydia got out her sewing kit. There was lace trim and wool flannel and bits of flowered cotton. Lydia sewed a dress and a coat, and a pair of pink shoes from a square of satin she'd saved over from dancing class.

Then didn't that doll shine like springtime! She gave the hair a rough little pat and put her back into her shoe box.

"Good night, Ugly Old Thing," she said.

But the doll didn't seem to belong in a box.

Lydia sat her on the bureau. To her right was a jar full of copper pennies. To her left sat a stack of old magazines. The scrap doll just smiled and stared out the window. She looked like a girl all alone at a party.

So Lydia took her down from the bureau.
She made a place for her head on the pillow.

Next morning, Lydia brought the doll down to breakfast.

"Look at those blue eyes," her mother said. "And that happy smile. Has she got a name?"

Lydia stopped eating, her spoon in mid-air. She looked surprised. "Her name is Sarah! I thought you knew."

Her mother smiled. "That's right," she said. "What a pretty name."

"It suits her," said Lydia, and went on eating.